HERCULES

THE TWELVE LABORS

A GREEK MYTH

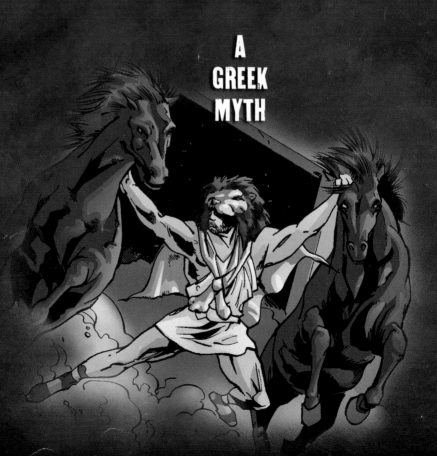

GRAPHIC UNIVERSE™

STORY BY
PAUL STORRIE

PENCILS BY
STEVE KURTH

INKS BY
BARBARA SCHULZ

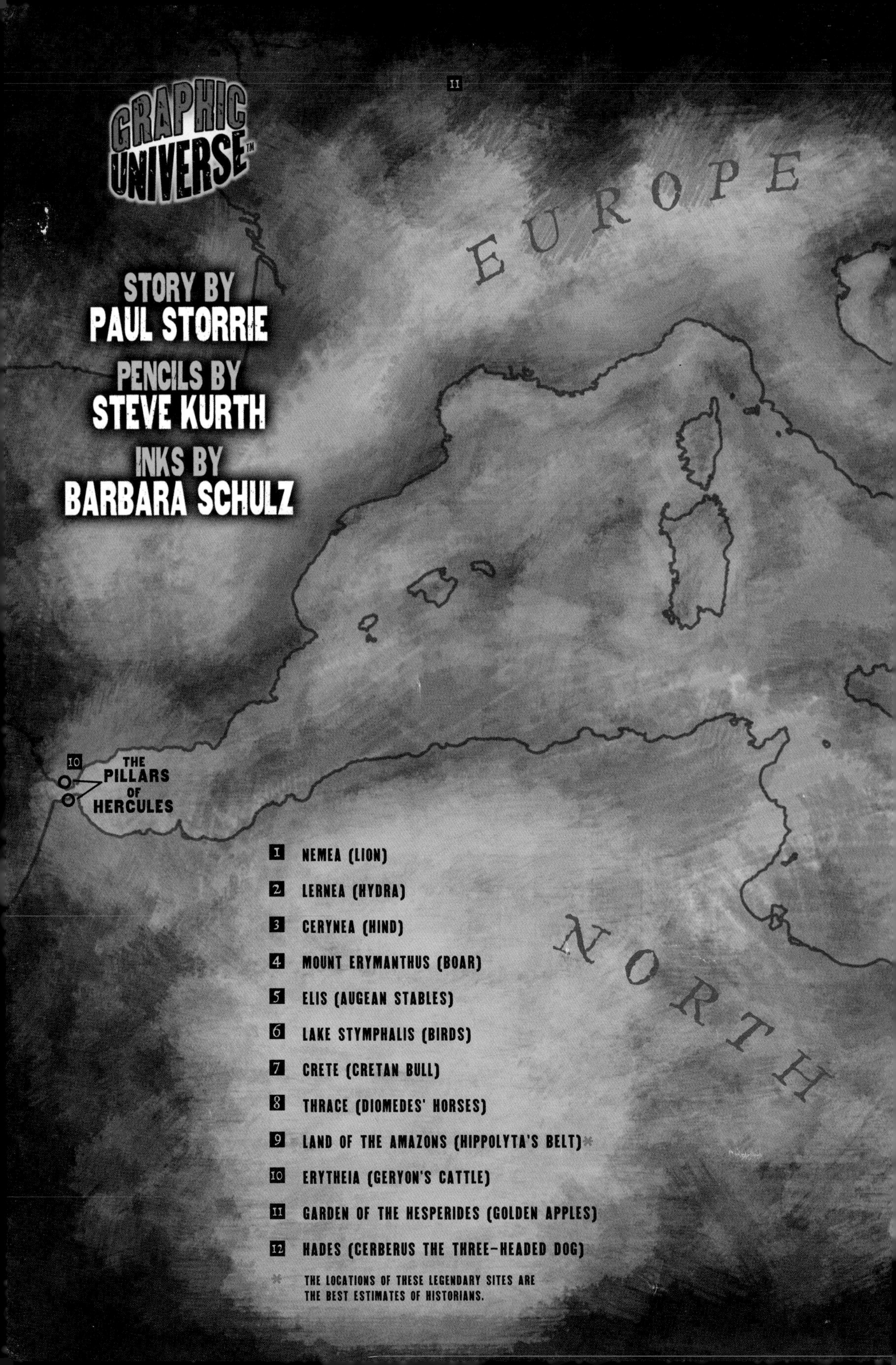

EUROPE

NORTH

10 THE
PILLARS
OF
HERCULES

1 NEMEA (LION)

2 LERNEA (HYDRA)

3 CERYNEA (HIND)

4 MOUNT ERYMANTHUS (BOAR)

5 ELIS (AUGEAN STABLES)

6 LAKE STYMPHALIS (BIRDS)

7 CRETE (CRETAN BULL)

8 THRACE (DIOMEDES' HORSES)

9 LAND OF THE AMAZONS (HIPPOLYTA'S BELT) ✳

10 ERYTHEIA (GERYON'S CATTLE)

11 GARDEN OF THE HESPERIDES (GOLDEN APPLES)

12 HADES (CERBERUS THE THREE-HEADED DOG)

✳ THE LOCATIONS OF THESE LEGENDARY SITES ARE
THE BEST ESTIMATES OF HISTORIANS.

HERCULES

THE TWELVE LABORS

A GREEK MYTH

8

9

GREECE

● MOUNT OLYMPUS

DELPHI

5 4 3 6 1 2 THEBES

MYCENAE

12

MEDITERRANEAN SEA

7

AFRICA

GRAPHIC UNIVERSE™ • MINNEAPOLIS

THE CHARACTER HERCULES MAY OR MAY NOT HAVE BEEN BASED ON AN ACTUAL PERSON. REGARDLESS, THE STORIES OF HIS GREAT FEATS OF STRENGTH, COURAGE, AND RESOURCEFULNESS ARE AMONG THE MOST FAMOUS GREEK LEGENDS. THE GREEKS CALLED THEIR GREATEST HERO HERAKLES. BUT THE ROMANS KNEW HIM AS HERCULES. THIS LATTER TITLE HAS COME DOWN THROUGH THE AGES AS THE MOST POPULAR NAME FOR THIS LARGER-THAN-LIFE FIGURE. TO CREATE THE STORY OF HERCULES' TWELVE LABORS, AUTHOR PAUL STORRIE RELIED HEAVILY ON BOTH THOMAS BULFINCH'S *THE AGE OF FABLE*, FIRST PUBLISHED IN 1859, AND EDITH HAMILTON'S *MYTHOLOGY*, FIRST PUBLISHED IN 1942. BOTH OF THESE DREW THEIR MATERIAL FROM THE WORK OF ANCIENT POETS SUCH AS OVID AND VIRGIL. ARTIST STEVE KURTH USED NUMEROUS HISTORICAL AND TRADITIONAL SOURCES TO GIVE THE ART AN AUTHENTIC FEEL, FROM THE CLASSICAL GREEK ARCHITECTURE TO THE CLOTHING, WEAPONS AND ARMOR WORN BY THE CHARACTERS.

STORY BY PAUL STORRIE

PENCILS BY STEVE KURTH
INKS BY BARBARA SCHULZ

COLORING BY HI-FI DESIGN

LETTERING BY BILL HAUSER

Copyright © 2007 by Lerner Publications Company

Graphic Universe™ is a trademark of Millbrook Press, Inc.

Graphic Universe™
An imprint of Lerner Publishing Group
241 First Avenue North
Minneapolis, MN 55401 U.S.A.

Website address: www.lernerbooks.com

Library of Congress Cataloging-in-Publication Data

Storrie, Paul D.
    Hercules : the Twelve Labors / by Paul Storrie ;
illustrations by Steve Kurth.
        p.   cm. — (Graphic myths and legends)
    ISBN-13: 978-0-8225-3084-8 (lib. bdg. : alk. paper)
    ISBN-10: 0-8225-3084-8 (lib. bdg. : alk. paper)
        1. Heracles (Greek mythology)—Juvenile literature.
I. Kurth, Steve. II. Title. III. Series: Graphic myths
and legends (Minneapolis, Minn.)
BL820.H5S86 2007
398.2'0938'02—dc22   2005023617

Manufactured in the United States of America
2 3 4 5 6 7 – JR – 12 11 10 09 08 07

TABLE OF CONTENTS

THE LEGEND BEGINS

LONG AGO, IN THE FAR OFF LAND OF GREECE, THERE LIVED A HERO NAMED **HERCULES**. THERE HAS NEVER BEEN A MAN AS STRONG, BEFORE OR SINCE.

HIS MOTHER WAS **ALCMENA**, A **MORTAL**, BUT HIS FATHER WAS **ZEUS**, THE KING OF THE **GODS**.

THE **GODDESS HERA** WAS JEALOUS THAT **ZEUS**, HER HUSBAND, LOVED A **MORTAL** WOMAN. BECAUSE OF THAT, SHE HATED **HERCULES**.

HERCULES WAS RAISED IN THE CITY OF *THEBES*, ALONG WITH HIS HALF BROTHER, *IPHICLES*.

ONE NIGHT, HERA SENT TWO SERPENTS TO SLAY THE SLEEPING HERCULES, NOT CARING THAT HIS BROTHER WAS IN DANGER TOO.

EACH NIGHT, *ALCMENA* WOULD PUT HER SONS TO BED IN A GREAT *BRONZE SHIELD* THAT SERVED AS THEIR CRIB.

BUT *ZEUS* WATCHED OVER HIS SON AND SENT A *BRIGHT LIGHT* TO WAKE HIM.

EVEN AS A *CHILD*, HE WAS *STRONG* ENOUGH TO SAVE HIS BROTHER AND HIMSELF.

SON OF *ZEUS*, YOU MUST GO TO YOUR COUSIN, *KING EURYSTHEUS* OF *MYCENAE*, AND PUT YOURSELF IN HIS SERVICE.

THIS IS THE WILL OF THE GODS.

WHEN HE WAS A GROWN MAN, HE WENT TO THE *ORACLE AT DELPHI*, WHO GAVE MESSAGES FROM THE *GODS*, TO LEARN WHAT HE SHOULD DO WITH HIS GREAT GIFT OF *STRENGTH*.

THOUGH *HERCULES* COULD NOT SEE HER, IT WAS THE *GODDESS* WHO SPOKE THROUGH ORACLE THAT DAY.

7

HAS THERE BEEN NO WORD?

SURELY THE BEAST HAS DEVOURED HIM BY NOW.

NO WORD YET MY KING, BUT...

EURYSTHEUS!

AAAHHH!

HA, HA, HA! HA!

NO NEED FOR FEAR, COUSIN!

DO YOU LIKE MY NEW CLOAK? IT WAS NOT EASY TO GET.

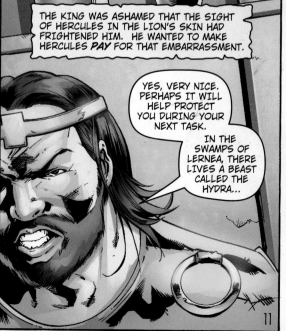

THE KING WAS ASHAMED THAT THE SIGHT OF HERCULES IN THE LION'S SKIN HAD FRIGHTENED HIM. HE WANTED TO MAKE HERCULES *PAY* FOR THAT EMBARRASSMENT.

YES, VERY NICE. PERHAPS IT WILL HELP PROTECT YOU DURING YOUR NEXT TASK.

IN THE SWAMPS OF LERNEA, THERE LIVES A BEAST CALLED THE HYDRA...

11

TO BEGIN HIS *SECOND LABOR* AS SOON AS POSSIBLE, HERCULES ASKED HIS NEPHEW *IOLAUS* TO TAKE HIM TO LERNEA BY CHARIOT. *IOLAUS* WAS THE SON OF *IPHICLES*, HERCULES' HALF BROTHER.

MUCH BETTER. HARD TO FIGHT WHAT YOU CAN BARELY SEE.

IS IT TRUE THAT THIS HYDRA HAS NINE HEADS, HERCULES? AND THAT ONE OF THE HEADS CANNOT BE KILLED?

SO EURYSTHEUS TELLS ME. AND THAT ITS BLOOD IS POISON.

I WONDER IF THERE WAS ANYTHING HE DECIDED NOT TO TELL?

LET'S SEE IF WE CAN ROUSE THE BEAST.

HISSSSSSSSSSSSSSSSSsssSSSSSSSsssSSSSSSsssSSsSsSs

THIS CANNOT BE! EACH HEAD I DESTROY, TWO TAKE ITS PLACE!

IOLAUS! GRAB A BRANCH FROM THE FIRE.

DRY!

IOLAUS?

I UNDERSTAND!

TSSSSS!

WHAT WERE YOU *THINKING*, HERCULES? TO TAKE A BOY HIS AGE INTO SUCH DANGER!

BESIDES, THE GODS' WISH WAS FOR *YOU* TO SERVE ME, NOT HAVE *IOLAUS* PERFORM YOUR LABORS FOR YOU!

HE ALREADY HAS A WARRIOR'S *COURAGE*. NOW HE MUST LEARN...

NO MATTER. YOUR *THIRD LABOR* WILL BE LESS CHALLENGING, SO YOU WILL HAVE NO NEED OF *HELP*.

I WANT YOU TO FETCH ME THE CERYNEAN HIND. AMAZING CREATURE -- IT HAS HORNS OF *GOLD*!

YOU WANT ME TO BRING YOU A DEER? HARDLY A LABOR TO MATCH MY PROWESS.

THIS SHOULD NOT TAKE LONG.

BUT YOU TOLD HIM...

I TOLD HIM TO *FETCH* THE ANIMAL, NOT HARM IT.

AH, YES. VERY CLEVER INDEED.

I ADMIT, I DO NOT UNDERSTAND EITHER. A HIND?

ONE SACRED TO THE MOON GODDESS *ARTEMIS*. IF HE KILLS IT, SHE WILL *SURELY* PUNISH HIM.

15

MONTHS LATER, HERCULES RETURNED.

EURYSTHEUS!

HERE IT IS!

HOW...? WHAT ABOUT...?

LONG MONTHS I TRACKED AND CHASED HER. SHE WAS FAST AND CLEVER. I THOUGHT I MIGHT NEVER CATCH HER.

FINALLY, I USED AN *ARROW* TO BRING HER DOWN.

THEN, AS I MADE MY WAY BACK, ARTEMIS APPEARED BEFORE ME!

SEEMS THIS GOLDEN-HORNED CREATURE IS A FAVORITE OF HERS.

SHE WAS ANGRY JUST *THINKING* THAT I HAD HURT IT.

HOW IS IT SHE LET YOU PASS, UNHINDERED AND UNHARMED?

LUCKY FOR ME, I HAD *NOT* HURT IT.

I KNEW SUCH A MAGNIFICENT CREATURE MUST BE TOUCHED BY THE GODS.

BUT YOU SAID...

THAT I BROUGHT IT DOWN WITH AN ARROW. I SHOT BETWEEN ITS LEGS AND TRIPPED IT. THEN I CAUGHT IT BEFORE IT COULD RUN.

SINCE IT WAS NOT HURT, ARTEMIS LET ME FINISH MY TASK. I HAD TO PROMISE TO LET IT GO. NOW I HAVE!

LATER...

WHAT TROUBLES YOU, MY KING?

Bah. IT IS ONLY A MATTER OF TIME BEFORE HERCULES RETURNS FROM HIS *FOURTH LABOR.*

SLAYING THE ERYMANTHEAN BOAR WILL BE NO CHALLENGE TO HIM.

PERHAPS NOT, MY KING.

BUT THE FEARSOME BOAR HAS BEEN TERRORIZING THOSE WHO LIVE NEAR MOUNT ERYMANTHUS.

AT LEAST IT WILL NO LONGER HURT YOUR PEOPLE.

TRUE. I JUST WISH I COULD THINK OF SOME OTHER LABOR TO...

KING EURYSTHEUS!

HERCULES IS COMING!

IT IS AMAZING, MY KING.

HE CHASED THE BEAST UP AND DOWN THE MOUNTAINSIDE FOR DAYS.

FINALLY, HE DROVE IT INTO A SNOWBANK NEAR THE PEAK.

THEN HE WAITED UNTIL IT WAS EXHAUSTED FROM STRUGGLING TO GET FREE!

EXHAUSTED?!? THEN IT IS STILL *ALIVE?!?*

Y-YES, MY KING.

AND HE IS *BRINGING* IT *HERE?*

YES, MY KING.

GO! RUN! TELL HERCULES THAT FROM NOW ON HE SHOULD SHOW THE PROOF OF HIS LABORS TO THE GUARD CAPTAIN AT THE GATE.

NOT TO ME, YOU UNDERSTAND? *NOT TO ME!*

17

GREAT CHALLENGES

KING EURYSTHEUS WAS ASHAMED AT BEING SO FRIGHTENED ABOUT THE BOAR. HE BLAMED HERCULES AND WANTED TO EMBARRASS HIS COUSIN JUST AS MUCH.

FOR THE *FIFTH LABOR*, EURYSTHEUS SENT HERCULES TO CLEAN OUT THE STABLES OF KING AUGEAS IN A SINGLE DAY, A TASK AS IMPOSSIBLE AS IT WAS DISGUSTING.

THERE THEY ARE -- THE STABLES THAT YOU AGREED TO CLEAN!

Ugh! BY THE SMELL, I CAN TELL NO ONE HAS TOUCHED THEM IN *YEARS*.

I WILL DO IT, BUT YOU MUST GIVE ME ONE OF EVERY TEN ANIMALS IN RETURN.

HA! WHY NOT?

TELL ME, PHYLEUS, MY SON, DO YOU THINK HE'LL MANAGE IT?

I DON'T KNOW, FATHER.

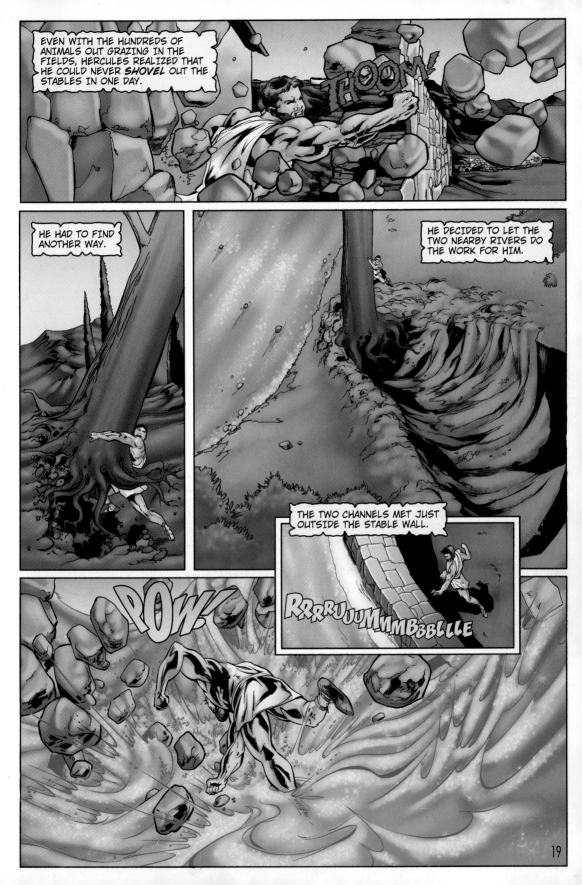

EVEN WITH THE HUNDREDS OF ANIMALS OUT GRAZING IN THE FIELDS, HERCULES REALIZED THAT HE COULD NEVER *SHOVEL* OUT THE STABLES IN ONE DAY.

THOOM!

HE HAD TO FIND ANOTHER WAY.

HE DECIDED TO LET THE TWO NEARBY RIVERS DO THE WORK FOR HIM.

THE TWO CHANNELS MET JUST OUTSIDE THE STABLE WALL.

POW!

RRRRUUMMMBBBLLLE

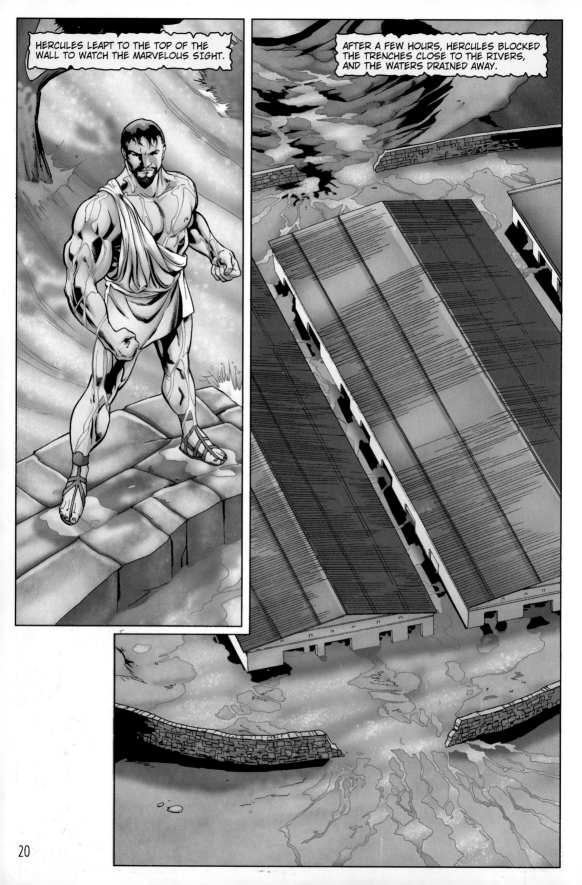

HERCULES LEAPT TO THE TOP OF THE WALL TO WATCH THE MARVELOUS SIGHT.

AFTER A FEW HOURS, HERCULES BLOCKED THE TRENCHES CLOSE TO THE RIVERS, AND THE WATERS DRAINED AWAY.

ARE YOU **INSANE?!?**

I HAVE DONE WHAT I SAID I WOULD DO. TIME TO PAY UP!

NO, IT IS NOT!

I HAVE LEARNED THAT YOU DID THIS AT THE BIDDING OF KING EURYSTHEUS AND THAT THE GODS TOLD YOU TO SERVE HIM. YOU HAD NO RIGHT TO ASK FOR PAYMENT!

WHATEVER HIS REASON, YOU PROMISED HIM THE ANIMALS, FATHER...

WHAT? YOU TAKE **HIS** SIDE?

GET OUT OF MY KINGDOM, THE PAIR OF YOU! COUNT YOURSELVES **LUCKY** TO LEAVE WITH YOUR **LIVES!**

DON'T WORRY, PHYLEUS. YOU'VE DONE NOTHING WRONG. SOMEDAY, YOU WILL INHERIT THE KINGDOM AS YOU SHOULD.

FOR NOW, YOU MUST COME WITH ME TO MYCENAE. THE LOOK ON **EURYSTHEUS'S** FACE WHEN HE LEARNS I COMPLETED HIS TASK **WITHOUT** WADING IN FILTH WILL RAISE YOUR SPIRITS!

21

THIS SHOULD ROUSE THEM.

AH! HERE THEY COME.

CLANG!

CLANG!

CLANG!

CLANG!

TAK TAK TAK TAK TAK TAK TAK TAK TAK TAK TAK TAK TAK

ARRGH!

ENOUGH OF THIS!

KREEE!

Think!

WHISS scech

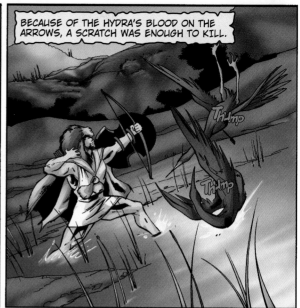

BECAUSE OF THE HYDRA'S BLOOD ON THE ARROWS, A SCRATCH WAS ENOUGH TO KILL.

Thimp

Thimp

HERCULES FIRED ARROW AFTER ARROW.

KREEE!

HIS ONLY FEAR WAS THAT HE WOULD NOT HAVE ENOUGH.

EVENTUALLY, THE LAST FEW BIRDS FLEW OFF. WHAT HAPPENED TO THEM, NO ONE KNOWS, BUT THEY NEVER RETURNED TO THE STYMPHALIAN LAKE AGAIN.

SOON, HERCULES FOUND THE BULL.

MRRRUUUUH!

THEY STRUGGLED FOR HOURS.

FINALLY, THE CREATURE BEGAN TO TIRE.

WHAM!

THE BULL HIT THE GROUND SO HARD THAT IT WAS DAZED.

Ugh! THANK THE GODS I DO NOT HAVE TO FIGHT YOU ALL THE WAY BACK TO THE SHIP!

AFTER HERCULES DELIVERED THE WHITE BULL OF CRETE, KING EURYSTHEUS SENT HIM TO THRACE TO STEAL AWAY A PAIR OF PRIZE MARES OWNED BY KING DIOMEDES. HIS *EIGHTH LABOR* SOUNDED EASY ENOUGH, BUT HERCULES HAD LEARNED TO EXPECT UNPLEASANT SURPRISES.

GREETINGS, FRIEND!

ARE THESE THE STABLES OF KING DIOMEDES?

YES, THEY ARE. YOU MUST NOT BE FROM THRACE. ALL THE LOCALS STAY AWAY.

WHY IS THAT? I HEAR THE MARES THAT DRAW THE KING'S CHARIOT ARE AMAZING CREATURES.

SO YOU CAME TO SEE THEM?

INDEED I DID.

SORRY, BUT THAT WOULD NOT BE SAFE. TRUST ME, I AM THEIR TRAINER.

YOU SOUND UNHAPPY ABOUT IT.

THE KING LIKES THEM TRAINED AND FED A CERTAIN WAY. IT MAKES THEM DANGEROUS.

FOR EXAMPLE, MOST HORSES LIKE TO BE PETTED. THESE WOULD HAPPILY GNAW YOUR HAND OFF.

GOOD TO KNOW.

TO BE HONEST, I WAS SENT HERE TO STEAL THEM.

I DID NOT LIKE THE IDEA, BUT IT SOUNDS LIKE DIOMEDES IS NOT FIT TO OWN THEM. I HOPE YOU WILL NOT TRY TO STOP ME.

I DOUBT I COULD, EVEN IF I WANTED TO. GOOD LUCK TO YOU. THEY WILL BE BETTER OFF AWAY FROM HERE.

CRUNCH!

THE TWO OF YOU ARE EVERY BIT AS NASTY AS YOUR TRAINER SAYS!

CRACK! CRACK!

SETTLE DOWN. YOU WILL GET NO TASTE OF ME.

THIEF!

THEY CAN HAVE YOU WHEN I FINISH!

TO DEFEND HIMSELF, HERCULES WAS FORCED TO RELEASE THE MARES.

No.

NOooooooooooor

SORRY. HE STRUCK ME WHEN I TRIED TO STOP HIM.

NO MATTER. IN THE END, HE GOT WHAT HE DESERVED.

PERHAPS. WILL EURYSTHEUS TREAT THEM BETTER?

I WILL TELL HIM WHAT HAPPENED TO DIOMEDES. IF I KNOW EURYSTHEUS, HE WILL BE TOO FRIGHTENED TO BE CRUEL TO THEM.

WHAT NOW? HERCULES HAS SUCCEEDED AT EVERY TASK I GAVE HIM. NOTHING HURTS HIM. NOTHING SHAMES HIM.

BUT WHAT...

YES! CALL FOR HERCULES!

FOR THE **NINTH LABOR**, KING EURYSTHEUS SENT HERCULES TO THE LAND OF THE AMAZONS. THE AMAZONS WERE A NATION OF FIERCE WARRIOR WOMEN WHO COULD FIGHT AS WELL AS ANY MAN. THE BRAVEST OF THEM, HIPPOLYTA, WAS THEIR QUEEN.

WHAT IS YOUR PURPOSE HERE?

I MUST SPEAK WITH HIPPOLYTA.

WHETHER YOU DO OR NOT WILL BE UP TO THE **QUEEN.**

I WILL BRING HER YOUR REQUEST.

UNTIL I RETURN, STAY ON YOUR SHIP.

IF YOU TRY TO COME ON LAND, MY COMRADES WILL STOP YOU.

A SHORT TIME LATER, THE QUEEN ARRIVED.

HAIL, HIPPOLYTA, QUEEN OF THE AMAZONS!

HAIL, HERCULES, HERO OF THEBES. WHY HAVE YOU MADE THE LONG JOURNEY TO MY LAND?

BY THE GODS' WILL, I SERVE MY COUSIN, KING EURYSTHEUS OF MYCENAE.

HE HAS *COMMANDED* THAT I BRING HIM THE GOLDEN BELT YOU WEAR.

YOU PLAN TO *TAKE* IT FROM ME? DO YOU THINK I WILL NOT *FIGHT* TO KEEP IT?

IT WAS A GIFT FROM ARES, THE GOD OF WAR.

I HOPE TO *PERSUADE* YOU TO PART WITH IT. I RESPECT YOU AND YOUR WARRIORS.

I DO NOT WISH TO BE YOUR ENEMY.

HAD YOU TRIED TO *TAKE* IT, I WOULD NEVER HAVE GIVEN IT UP.

BECAUSE YOU *ASKED* AND BECAUSE OF THE RESPECT I HAVE FOR YOU AND YOUR ADVENTURES, I WILL GIVE IT TO YOU AS A TOKEN OF FRIENDSHIP.

31

ONCE AGAIN, HERA WAS NEARBY, WATCHING AND HOPING THAT HERCULES WOULD FAIL. WHEN SHE SAW THE QUEEN GIVE UP THE BELT WITHOUT A FIGHT, HERA DISGUISED HERSELF AS AN AMAZON TO MAKE TROUBLE.

LOOK! HERCULES MUST HAVE TAKEN THE QUEEN *HOSTAGE!*

WHY ELSE WOULD SHE SURRENDER SUCH A TREASURE?

YES! YOU MUST BE RIGHT!

WE MUST STOP THEM BEFORE THEY SET SAIL!

STOP THEM!!!

ATTACK!!

WHAT IS THIS?!? YOU SPEAK OF *FRIENDSHIP* AND THEN YOUR WARRIORS *ATTACK?*

MY WARRIORS WOULD ONLY *ATTACK* IF THEY SAW SOME *TREACHERY!*

I SHOULD HAVE KNOWN BETTER THAN TO TRUST A *MAN!*

SAVE THE QUEEN!

STOP THEM!!

GET THEM!

32

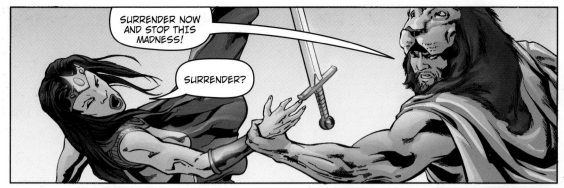

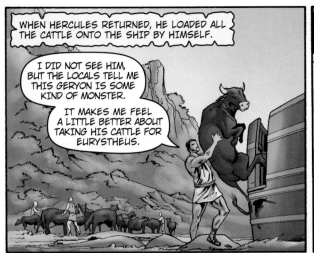

WHEN HERCULES RETURNED, HE LOADED ALL THE CATTLE ONTO THE SHIP BY HIMSELF.

I DID NOT SEE HIM, BUT THE LOCALS TELL ME THIS GERYON IS SOME KIND OF MONSTER.

IT MAKES ME FEEL A LITTLE BETTER ABOUT TAKING HIS CATTLE FOR EURYSTHEUS.

RRRaaaaaaRRRrr!!

YOU'VE TAKEN MY CATTLE!

I'LL KILL YOU ALL!!

GET MY BOW! NOW!

35

NOoOOOo!!!

WHIST

ARRGGHHH!

YOU KILLED HIM WITH A POISONED ARROW? I AM **SURPRISED**, HERCULES.

YOU ARE A MIGHTY WARRIOR. WHY NOT FIGHT IT FAIRLY?

I THOUGHT ABOUT IT. THEN IT OCCURRED TO ME THAT YOU, YOUR CREW, AND YOUR SHIP MIGHT GET SMASHED TO PIECES IN THE FIGHT.

oh.

ABOVE AND BELOW

FOR THE **ELEVENTH LABOR**, KING EURYSTHEUS SENT HERCULES TO BRING HIM THE GOLDEN APPLES OF THE HESPERIDES, WHICH BELONGED TO HERA. THE GODDESS WHISPERED THE SUGGESTION TO THE KING BECAUSE SHE THOUGHT THE CHALLENGE WOULD BE IMPOSSIBLE.

FIRST, EVERYONE KNEW THAT THE HESPERIDES, THE FOUR NYMPHS WHO CARED FOR THE TREE OF GOLDEN APPLES AND THE GARDEN WHERE IT GREW, GUARDED IT CAREFULLY. SECOND, NO ONE KNEW EXACTLY WHERE THE GARDEN WAS.

BUT HERCULES KNEW THAT ATLAS, THE TITAN WHO HELD UP THE SKY, WAS RELATED TO THE NYMPHS. IF ANYONE WOULD KNOW HOW TO FIND THEM, IT WOULD BE ATLAS. SO HERCULES MADE THE LONG, DANGEROUS CLIMB TO ASK HIM.

HA! I CANNOT REMEMBER THE LAST TIME SOMEONE CAME TO VISIT ME HERE.

OF COURSE, MY HOME IS NOT TOO INVITING.

WHO ARE YOU? WHY HAVE YOU COME?

I AM HERCULES. I HAVE COME FOR YOUR HELP.

I WAS TOLD TO GET SOME OF THE GOLDEN APPLES THAT THE HESPERIDES WATCH OVER.

TELL ME WHERE TO FIND THEM.

EVERY HOUR THAT HE STRAINED TO HOLD THE SKY FELT LIKE A YEAR TO HERCULES. HE WAS GLAD TO SEE THE TITAN RETURN.

HERE THEY ARE! VERY PRETTY. EURYSTHEUS WILL LIKE THEM.

YES, I THINK SO TOO. NOW, TAKE BACK THE SKY.

NO. NO, I THINK NOT. I HAVE HELD THE SKY FOR LONG ENOUGH. YOU CAN HOLD IT FROM NOW ON.

REMEMBER, I PROMISED TO BRING THE APPLES HERE. I NEVER SAID I WOULD TAKE BACK THE SKY.

WHAT?!?

DO NOT WORRY. I WILL TAKE THE APPLES TO EURYSTHEUS FOR YOU.

THANK YOU FOR THAT.

YOU HAVE BEEN HOLDING THE SKY MANY YEARS. I SUPPOSE IT IS ONLY FAIR THAT SOMEONE ELSE DO IT FOR A WHILE.

I WONDER IF YOU CAN DO ME A FAVOR, THOUGH?

CAN YOU TAKE BACK THE SKY FOR A TIME?

IF I FOLD MY CLOAK INTO A PAD FOR MY SHOULDERS I WOULD BE MORE COMFORTABLE.

HMMM. I SUPPOSE.

A PAD WOULD HAVE BEEN NICE ALL THOSE YEARS I WAS HOLDING THE SKY.

THE MONSTROUS CERBERUS, GUARDIAN OF THE GATES OF THE UNDERWORLD, MADE SURE THAT NO ONE ESCAPED BACK INTO THE LAND OF THE LIVING.

AS HERCULES PASSED BY, HE KNEW HE MIGHT NEVER SEE THE WORLD ABOVE AGAIN.

ALONG TWISTING PATHS, HE MADE HIS WAY TO THE COURT OF HADES, LORD OF THE DEAD.

AH. I KNEW THAT A LIVING MAN HAD ENTERED MY REALM, BUT I DID NOT REALIZE THAT IT WAS YOU.

WELCOME, SON OF MY BROTHER ZEUS. WHY ARE *YOU* HERE?

I COME BECAUSE THE ORACLE AT DELPHI PUT ME IN THE SERVICE OF EURYSTHEUS.

HE COMMANDED ME TO BRING HIM CERBERUS.

DID HE? I THINK I SEE HERA'S HAND IN THIS. SHE NEVER LIKED YOU. SHE THINKS I WILL NOT LET YOU GO.

BECAUSE OF THAT, AND BECAUSE I DO NOT WANT TO ANGER ZEUS, I THINK I WILL LET YOU RETURN TO THE LAND OF THE LIVING.

THANK YOU, GREAT HADES.

WILL YOU LET ME COMPLETE MY TASK? CAN I TAKE CERBERUS WITH ME?

SINCE YOU ARE OBEYING THE ORACLE, I WILL ALLOW YOU TO TAKE CERBERUS...

BUT ONLY IF YOU CAN TAME HIM WITH YOUR BARE HANDS.

OH, AND TELL EURYSTHEUS THAT YOUR SERVICE IS AT AN END. TELL HIM I SAID SO.

GRRRRrrrrrr

AAIIIEEEEE!

NOW, RETURN TO YOUR MASTER.

I HAVE COMPLETED THE TWELFTH LABOR YOU GAVE ME.

NOW MY SERVICE TO YOU IS FINISHED.

THAT WAS THE END OF THE TWELVE LABORS OF HERCULES, BUT THAT WAS NOT THE END OF HIS ADVENTURES.

ALL HIS LIFE, HERCULES NEVER STOPPED MAKING DANGEROUS JOURNEYS AND FIGHTING AGAINST FEARSOME ENEMIES, BUT THOSE ARE STORIES FOR ANOTHER TIME.

GLOSSARY

AMAZONS: a race of female warriors of Greek legend. Hippolyta, daughter of the god of war—Ares—is the queen of the Amazons.

ARTEMIS: the Greek goddess of the moon and of the hunt

BOAR: a male pig

HADES: the underground dwelling place of the dead in Greek mythology

HERA: the immortal wife of Zeus

HIDE: the skin of an animal

HIND: a female deer

IMMORTAL: a being that never dies

MARE: a female horse

MORTAL: a being that dies

NYMPH: in Greek mythology, goddesses of nature who are often represented as beautiful women living in the mountains, forests, trees, and waters

ORACLE: a priestess of ancient Greece through whom a god or gods were believed to speak

POSEIDON: the Greek god of the sea

TITAN: according to Greek mythology, a race of giants that ruled the earth before their overthrow by the Greek gods

ZEUS: king of the gods, father of Hercules

pencil from page 45

46

FURTHER READING AND WEBSITES

Greek Mythology: The Labors of Hercules
http://www.mythweb.com/hercules/index.html
>   With engaging cartoons and easy-to-read text, this kid-friendly site explores
>   the labors of Hercules and also tells the stories of several other Greek heroes.

Hamilton, Edith. *Mythology*. New York: Warner Books, Inc., 1999.
>   First published in 1942, this classic work is a collection of lively retellings of
>   Greek, Roman, and Norse tales.

Perseus Project: Hercules: Greece's Greatest Hero
http://www.perseus.tufts.edu/Herakles/index.html
>   This website from Tufts University in Massachusetts features a wealth of
>   information about the legend of Hercules, including his twelve labors and
>   other stories.

Philip, Neil. *Mythology*. New York: Dorling Kindersley, 1999.
>   This volume in the Eyewitness Books series uses dozens of colorful photos and
>   illustrations to explore myths from around the world.

Roberts, Morgan J. *Classical Deities and Heroes*. New York: Metro Books, 1995.
>   Filled with colorful illustrations and photos of ancient artifacts, this book
>   recounts many of the most popular Greek and Roman myths, including the
>   twelve labors of Hercules.

Thomas Bulfinch: Bulfinch's Mythology
http://www.classicreader.com/booktoc.php/sid.2/bookid.2823/
>   This website features one of the most popular English-language compilations
>   of ancient myths. This classic work, which includes many Greek myths, was
>   compiled by American Thomas Bulfinch in the 1800s.

CREATING HERCULES: THE TWELVE LABORS

To create the story of Hercules' Twelve Labors, author Paul Storrie relied
heavily on both Thomas Bulfinch's *The Age of Fable*, first published in 1859, and
Edith Hamilton's *Mythology*, first published in 1942. Both of these drew their
material from the work of ancient poets such as Ovid and Virgil. Artist Steve
Kurth used numerous historical and traditional sources to give the art an authentic
feel, from the classical Greek architecture to the clothing, weapons and armor
worn by the characters. Together, the art and narrative text bring to life the
mightiest hero of Greek myth, whose battles against gods and monsters earned him
a place on Mt. Olympus, the home of the Greek gods.

INDEX

ABOUT THE AUTHOR AND THE ARTIST

PAUL D. STORRIE was born and raised in Detroit, Michigan and has returned to live there again and again after living in other cities and states. He began writing professionally in 1987 and has written comics for Caliber Comics, Moonstone Books, Marvel Comics and DC Comics. Some of the titles he's worked on include *Robyn of Sherwood*, featuring stories about Robin Hood's daughter, *Batman Beyond*, *Gotham Girls*, *Captain America: Red, White and Blue* and *Mutant X*.

STEVE KURTH was born and raised in west central Wisconsin. He graduated with a bachelor's degree in fine arts in illustration from the University Wisconsin at Eau Claire. Steve's art has appeared in numerous comic books, including *G.I. Joe*, *Micronauts*, *Ghostbusters*, *Dragonlance*, and *Cracked* magazine.

Health Reference Series

1998-1999

Health Reference Series

The Complete Consumer Health Collection for the General Reader . . .

- 58 subject volumes
- Easy-to-understand format
- Non-technical language
- For patients, families, and caregivers

66 Public and academic libraries . . .
will want to consider Omnigraphics'
Health Reference Series. " — *Booklist, Nov '95* 99

by
Omnigraphics, Inc.

Health Reference Series

The Complete Consumer Health Collection for the General Reader . . .

- 58 subject volumes
- Easy-to-understand format
- Non-technical language
- For patients, families, and caregivers

Aging Body Sourcebook

Basic Information about Maintaining Health through the Post-Reproductive Years, Including a Description of the Aging Process, Physical Changes, Preventive Medicine, and Mental Health Issues for Seniors; Along with Statistical and Demographic Data, Recommended Lifestyle Modifications, a Glossary, and a List of Resources for Additional Help and Information

Ready March '99. Edited by Jenifer Swanson. Approx. 600 pages. 0-7808-0233-0. $78.

AIDS Sourcebook, 1st Edition

Basic Information about AIDS and HIV Infection, Featuring Historical and Statistical Data, Current Research, Prevention, and Other Special Topics of Interest for Persons Living with AIDS, Along with Source Listings for Further Assistance

In Print. Edited by Karen Bellenir and Peter D. Dresser. 831 pages. 1995. 0-7808-0031-1. $78.

"One strength of this book is its practical emphasis. The intended audience is the lay reader . . . useful as an educational tool for health care providers who work with AIDS patients. Recommended for public libraries as well as hospital or academic libraries that collect consumer materials." — *Bulletin of the MLA, Jan '96*

"This is the most comprehensive volume of its kind on an important medical topic. Highly recommended for all libraries." — *Reference Book Review, '96*

"Very useful reference for all libraries." — *Choice, Oct '95*

"There is a wealth of information here that can provide much educational assistance. It is a must book for all libraries and should be on the desk of each and every congressional leader. Highly recommended." — *AIDS Book Review Journal, Aug '95*

"Recommended for most collections." — *Library Journal, Jul '95*

AIDS Sourcebook, 2nd Edition

Basic Information about AIDS and HIV Infection, Featuring Updated Statistical Data, Research Reports, Prevention Initiatives, the Quest for a Vaccine, and Other Special Topics of Interest for Persons Living with AIDS Such as Treatment Options, Clinical Trials, and Health Insurance Coverage Issues, Along with a Glossary of Important Terms and Resource Listings for Further Help and Information

Ready January '99. Edited by Karen Bellenir. Approx. 600 pages. 0-7808-0225-X. $78.

Allergies Sourcebook

Basic Information about Major Forms and Mechanisms of Common Allergic Reactions, Sensitivities, and Intolerances, Including Anaphylaxis, Asthma, Hives and Other Dermatologic Symptoms, Rhinitis, and Sinusitis, Along with Their Usual Triggers Like Animal Fur, Chemicals, Drugs, Dust, Foods, Insects, Latex, Pollen, and Poison Ivy, Oak, and Sumac; Plus Information on Prevention, Identification, and Treatment

In Print. Edited by Allan R. Cook. 611 pages. 1997. 0-7808-0036-2. $78.

Alternative Medicine Sourcebook

Basic Information about Alternatives to Conventional Medicine, Including Acupressure, Acupuncture, Aromatherapy, Ayurveda, Bioelectromagnetics, Environmental Medicine, Essence Therapy, Food Therapy, Herbal Therapy, Homeopathy, Hydrotherapy, Imaging, Massage, Naturopathy, Reflexology, Relaxation and Meditation, Sound Therapy, Vitamin and Mineral Therapy, and Yoga

Ready January '99. Edited by Allan R. Cook. Approx. 600 pages. 0-7808-0200-4. $78.

Alzheimer's, Stroke & 29 Other Neurological Disorders Sourcebook, 1st Edition

Basic Information for the Layperson on 31 Diseases or Disorders Affecting the Brain and Nervous System, First Describing the Illness, Then Listing Symptoms, Diagnostic Methods, and Treatment Options, and Including Statistics on Incidences and Causes

In Print. Edited by Frank E. Bair. 579 pages. 1993. 1-55888-748-2. $78.

"Nontechnical reference book that provides reader-friendly information."
— *Family Caregiver Alliance Update, Winter '96*

". . . should be included in any library's patient education section."
— *American Reference Books Annual, '94*

"Written in an approachable and accessible style. Recommended for patient education and consumer health collections in health science center and public libraries." — *Academic Library Book Review, Dec '93*

"It is very handy to have information on more than thirty neurological disorders under one cover, and there is no recent source like it." — *RQ, Fall '93*

Alzheimer's Disease Sourcebook, 2nd Edition

Basic Information about Alzheimer's Disease, Related Disorders, and Other Dementias, Including Multi-Infarct Dementia, AIDS-Related Dementia, Alcoholic Dementia, Huntington's Disease, Delirium, and Confusional States; Along with Reports Detailing Current Research Efforts in Prevention and Treatment, Long-Term Care Issues, and Listings of Sources for Additional Help and Information

In Print. Edited by Karen Bellenir. 600 pages. 1998. 0-7808-0223-3. $78.

Arthritis Sourcebook

Basic Consumer Health Information about Specific Forms of Arthritis and Related Disorders, Including Rheumatoid Arthritis, Osteoarthritis, Gout, Polymyalgia Rheumatica, Psoriatic Arthritis, Spondyloarthropathies, Juvenile Rheumatoid Arthritis, and Juvenile Ankylosing Spondylitis; Along with Information about Medical, Surgical, and Alternative Treatment Options, and Including Strategies for Coping with Pain, Fatigue, and Stress

In Print. Edited by Allan R. Cook. 575 pages. 1998. 0-7808-0201-2. $78.

Back & Neck Disorders Sourcebook

Basic Information about Disorders and Injuries of the Spinal Cord and Vertebrae, Including Facts on Chiropractic Treatment, Surgical Interventions, Paralysis, and Rehabilitation, Along with Advice for Preventing Back Trouble

In Print. Edited by Karen Bellenir. 548 pages. 1997. 0-7808-0202-0. $78.

"The strength of this work is its basic, easy-to-read format. Recommended."
— *Reference and User Services Quarterly, Winter '97*

Blood & Circulatory Disorders Sourcebook

Basic Information about Blood and Its Components, Anemias, Leukemias, Bleeding Disorders, and Circulatory Disorders, Including Aplastic Anemia, Thalassemia, Sickle-Cell Disease, Hemochromatosis, Hemophilia, Von Willebrand Disease, and Vascular Diseases; Along with a Special Section on Blood Transfusions and Blood Supply Safety, a Glossary, and Source Listings for Further Help and Information

In Print. Edited by Karen Bellenir and Linda M. Shin. 575 pages. 1998. 0-7808-0203-9. $78.

Burns Sourcebook

Basic Information about Various Types of Burns and Scalds, Including Flame, Heat, Electrical, Chemical, and Sun; Along with Short- and Long-Term Treatments, Tissue Reconstruction, Plastic Surgery, Prevention Suggestions, and First Aid

Ready January '99. Edited by Allan R. Cook. Approx. 600 pages. 0-7808-0204-7. $78.

Cancer Sourcebook, 1st Edition

Basic Information on Cancer Types, Symptoms, Diagnostic Methods, and Treatments, Including Statistics on Cancer Occurrences Worldwide and the Risks Associated with Known Carcinogens and Activities

In Print. Edited by Frank E. Bair. 932 pages. 1990. 1-55888-888-8. $78.

"Written in nontechnical language. Useful for patients, their families, medical professionals, and librarians."
— *Guide to Reference Books, '96*

"Designed with the non-medical professional in mind. Libraries and medical facilities interested in patient education should certainly consider adding the *Cancer Sourcebook* to their holdings. This compact collection of reliable information, written in a positive, hopeful tone, is an invaluable tool for helping patients and patients' families and friends to take the first steps in coping with the many difficulties of cancer."
— *Medical Reference Services Quarterly, Winter '91*

"Specifically created for the nontechnical reader . . . an important resource for the general reader trying to understand the complexities of cancer."
— *American Reference Books Annual, '91*

"This publication's nontechnical nature and very comprehensive format make it useful for both the general public and undergraduate students."
— *Choice, Oct '90*

New Cancer Sourcebook, 2nd Edition

Basic Information about Major Forms and Stages of Cancer, Featuring Facts about Primary and Secondary Tumors of the Respiratory, Nervous, Lymphatic, Circulatory, Skeletal, and Gastrointestinal Systems, and Specific Organs; Statistical and Demographic Data; Treatment Options; and Strategies for Coping

In Print. Edited by Allan R. Cook. 1,313 pages. 1996. 0-7808-0041-9. $78.

"This book is an excellent resource for patients with newly diagnosed cancer and their families. The dialogue is simple, direct, and comprehensive. Highly recommended for patients and families to aid in their understanding of cancer and its treatment"
— *Booklist Health Sciences Supplement, Oct '97*

"The amount of factual and useful information is extensive. The writing is very clear, geared to general readers. Recommended for all levels."
— *Choice, Jan '97*

Cancer Sourcebook, 3rd Edition

Basic Information about Major Forms and Stages of Cancer, Featuring Facts about Primary and Secondary Tumors of the Respiratory, Nervous, Lymphatic, Circulatory, Skeletal, and Gastrointestinal Systems, and Specific Organs, Statistical and Demographic Data, Treatment Options, and Strategies for Coping

Ready July '99. Edited by Edward J. Prucha. Approx. 800 pages. 0-7808-0227-6. $78.

Cancer Sourcebook for Women, 1st Edition

Basic Information about Specific Forms of Cancer That Affect Women, Featuring Facts about Breast Cancer, Cervical Cancer, Ovarian Cancer, Cancer of the Uterus and Uterine Sarcoma, Cancer of the Vagina, and Cancer of the Vulva; Statistical and Demographic Data; Treatments, Self-Help Management Suggestions, and Current Research Initiatives

In Print. Edited by Allan R. Cook and Peter D. Dresser. 524 pages. 1996. 0-7808-0076-1. $78.

". . . written in easily understandable, non-technical language. Recommended for public libraries or hospital and academic libraries that collect patient education or consumer health materials."
— *Medical Reference Services Quarterly, Spring '97*

"Would be of value in a consumer health library. . . . written with the health care consumer in mind. Medical jargon is at a minimum, and medical terms are explained in clear, understandable sentences."
— *Bulletin of the MLA, Oct '96*

"The availability under one cover of all these pertinent publications, grouped under cohesive headings, makes this certainly a most useful sourcebook."
— *Choice, Jun '96*

"Presents a comprehensive knowledge base for general readers. Men and women both benefit from the gold mine of information nestled between the two covers of this book. Recommended."
— *Academic Library Book Review, Summer '96*

"This timely book is highly recommended for consumer health and patient education collections in all libraries."
— *Library Journal, Apr '96*

Cancer Sourcebook for Women, 2nd Edition

Basic Information about Specific Forms of Cancer That Affect Women, Featuring Facts about Breast Cancer, Cervical Cancer, Ovarian Cancer, Cancer of the Uterus and Uterine Sarcoma, Cancer of the Vagina, and Cancer of the Vulva, Statistical and Demographic Data, Treatments, Self-Help Management Suggestions, and Current Research Initiatives

Ready June '99. Edited by Edward J. Prucha. Approx. 600 pages. 0-7808-0226-8. $78.

Cardiovascular Diseases & Disorders Sourcebook

Basic Information about Cardiovascular Diseases and Disorders, Featuring Facts about the Cardiovascular System, Demographic and Statistical Data, Descriptions of Pharmacological and Surgical Interventions, Lifestyle Modifications, and a Special Section Focusing on Heart Disorders in Children

In Print. Edited by Karen Bellenir and Peter D. Dresser. 683 pages. 1995. 0-7808-0032-X. $78.

". . . comprehensive format provides an extensive overview on this subject." — *Choice, Jun '96*

". . . an easily understood, complete, up-to-date resource. This well executed public health tool will make valuable information available to those that need it most, patients and their families. The typeface, sturdy non-reflective paper, and library binding add a feel of quality found wanting in other publications. Highly recommended for academic and general libraries." — *Academic Library Book Review, Summer '96*

Communication Disorders Sourcebook

Basic Information about Deafness and Hearing Loss, Speech and Language Disorders, Voice Disorders, Balance and Vestibular Disorders, and Disorders of Smell, Taste, and Touch

In Print. Edited by Linda M. Ross. 533 pages. 1996. 0-7808-0077-X. $78.

"This is skillfully edited and is a welcome resource for the layperson. It should be found in every public and medical library." — *Booklist Health Sciences Supplement, Oct '97*

Congenital Disorders Sourcebook

Basic Information about Disorders Acquired during Gestation, Including Spina Bifida, Hydrocephalus, Cerebral Palsy, Heart Defects, Craniofacial Abnormalities, Fetal Alcohol Syndrome, and More, Along with Current Treatment Options and Statistical Data

In Print. Edited by Karen Bellenir. 607 pages. 1997. 0-7808-0205-5. $78.

"Recommended reference source." — *Booklist, Oct '97*

Fax Orders: 800-875-1340
24 Hours a Day, 7 Days a Week

Consumer Issues in Health Care Sourcebook

Basic Information about Health Care Fundamentals and Related Consumer Issues, Including Exams and Screening Tests, Physician Specialties, Choosing a Doctor, Using Prescription and Over-the-Counter Medications Safely, Avoiding Health Scams, Managing Common Health Risks in the Home, Care Options for Chronically or Terminally Ill Patients, and a List of Resources for Obtaining Help and Further Information

In Print. Edited by Karen Bellenir. 592 pages. 1998. 0-7808-0221-7. $78.

Contagious & Non-Contagious Infectious Diseases Sourcebook

Basic Information about Contagious Diseases like Measles, Polio, Hepatitis B, and Infectious Mononucleosis, and Non-Contagious Infectious Diseases like Tetanus and Toxic Shock Syndrome, and Diseases Occurring as Secondary Infections Such as Shingles and Reye Syndrome, Along with Vaccination, Prevention, and Treatment Information, and a Section Describing Emerging Infectious Disease Threats

In Print. Edited by Karen Bellenir and Peter D. Dresser. 566 pages. 1996. 0-7808-0075-3. $78.

Death & Dying Sourcebook

Basic Information for the Layperson about End-of-Life Care and Related Ethical and Legal Issues, Including Chief Causes of Death, Autopsies, Pain Management for the Terminally Ill, Life Support Systems, Coma, Euthanasia, Assisted Suicide, Hospice Programs, Living Wills, Near-Death Experiences, Counseling, Mourning, Organ Donation, Cryogenics and Physician Training and Liability, Along with Statistical Data, a Glossary, and Listings of Sources for Additional Help and Information

Ready March '99. Edited by Annemarie Muth. Approx. 600 pages. 0-7808-0230-6. $78.

Diabetes Sourcebook, 1st Edition

Basic Information about Insulin-Dependent and Noninsulin-Dependent Diabetes Mellitus, Gestational Diabetes, and Diabetic Complications, Symptoms, Treatment, and Research Results, Including Statistics on Prevalence, Morbidity, and Mortality, Along with Source Listings for Further Help and Information

In Print. Edited by Karen Bellenir and Peter D. Dresser. 827 pages. 1994. 1-55888-751-2. $78.

". . . very informative and understandable for the layperson without being simplistic. It provides a comprehensive overview for laypersons who want a general understanding of the disease or who want to focus on various aspects of the disease." — *Bulletin of the MLA, Jan '96*

Diabetes Sourcebook, 2nd Edition

Basic Consumer Health Information about Type 1 Diabetes (Insulin-Dependent or Juvenile-Onset Diabetes), Type 2 (Noninsulin-Dependent or Adult-Onset Diabetes), Gestational Diabetes, and Related Disorders, Including Diabetes Prevalence Data, Management Issues, the Role of Diet and Exercise in Controlling Diabetes, Insulin and Other Diabetes Medicines, and Complications of Diabetes Such as Eye Diseases, Periodontal Disease, Amputation, and End-Stage Renal Disease; Along with Reports on Current Research Initiatives, a Glossary, and Resource Listings for Further Help and Information

In Print. Edited by Karen Bellenir. 725 pages. 1998. 0-7808-0224-1. $78.

Diet & Nutrition Sourcebook, 1st Edition

Basic Information about Nutrition, Including the Dietary Guidelines for Americans, the Food Guide Pyramid, and Their Applications in Daily Diet, Nutritional Advice for Specific Age Groups, Current Nutritional Issues and Controversies, the New Food Label and How to Use It to Promote Healthy Eating, and Recent Developments in Nutritional Research

In Print. Edited by Dan R. Harris. 662 pages. 1996. 0-7808-0084-2. $78.

"Useful reference as a food and nutrition sourcebook for the general consumer."
— *Booklist Health Sciences Supplement, Oct '97*

"Recommended for public libraries and medical libraries that receive general information requests on nutrition. It is readable and will appeal to those interested in learning more about healthy dietary practices."
— *Medical Reference Services Quarterly, Fall '97*

"An abundance of medical and social statistics is translated into readable information geared toward the general reader."
— *Bookwatch, Mar '97*

"With dozens of questionable diet books on the market, it is so refreshing to find a reliable and factual reference book. Recommended to aspiring professionals, librarians, and others seeking and giving reliable dietary advice. An excellent compilation."
— *Choice, Feb '97*

Diet & Nutrition Sourcebook, 2nd Edition

Basic Information about Nutrition, Including General Nutritional Recommendations, Recommendations for People with Specific Medical Concerns, Dieting for Weight Control, Nutritional Supplements, Food Safety Issues, the Relationship between Nutrition and Disease Development, and Other Nutritional Research Reports; Along with Statistical and Demographic Data, Lifestyle Modification Recommendations, and Sources of Additional Help and Information

Ready January '99. Edited by Karen Bellenir. Approx. 600 pages. 0-7808-0228-4. $78.

Domestic Violence Sourcebook

Basic Information about the Physical, Emotional and Sexual Abuse of Partners, Children, and Elders, Including Information about Hotlines, Safe Houses, Safety Plans, Resources for Support and Assistance, Community Initiatives, and Reports on Current Directions in Research and Treatment; Along with a Glossary, Sources for Further Reading, and Listings of Governmental and Non-Governmental Organizations

Ready February '99. Edited by Helene Henderson. Approx. 600 pages. 0-7808-0235-7. $78.

Ear, Nose & Throat Disorders Sourcebook

Basic Information about Disorders of the Ears, Nose, Sinus Cavities, Pharynx, and Larynx, Including Ear Infections, Tinnitus, Vestibular Disorders, Allergic and Non-Allergic Rhinitis, Sore Throats, Tonsillitis, and Cancers That Affect the Ears, Nose, Sinuses, and Throat, Along with Reports on Current Research Initiatives, a Glossary of Related Medical Terms, and a Directory of Sources for Further Help and Information

In Print. Edited by Karen Bellenir and Linda M. Shin. 592 pages. 1998. 0-7808-0206-3. $78.

Endocrine & Metabolic Disorders Sourcebook

Basic Information for the Layperson about Pancreatic and Insulin-Related Disorders Such as Pancreatitis, Diabetes, and Hypoglycemia; Adrenal Gland Disorders Such as Cushing's Syndrome, Addison's Disease, and Congenital Adrenal Hyperplasia; Pituitary Gland Disorders Such as Growth Hormone Deficiency, Acromegaly, and Pituitary Tumors; Thyroid Disorders Such as Hypothyroidism, Graves' Disease, Hashimoto's Disease, and Goiter; Hyperparathyroidism; and Other Diseases and Syndromes of Hormone Imbalance or Metabolic Dysfunction, Along with Reports on Current Research Initiatives

In Print. Edited by Linda M. Shin. 632 pages. 1998. 0-7808-0207-1. $78.

Environmentally Induced Disorders Sourcebook

Basic Information about Diseases and Syndromes Linked to Exposure to Pollutants and Other Substances in Outdoor and Indoor Environments Such as Lead, Asbestos, Formaldehyde, Mercury, Emissions, Noise, and More

In Print. Edited by Allan R. Cook. 620 pages. 1997. 0-7808-0083-4. $78.

". . . a good survey of numerous environmentally induced physical disorders . . . a useful addition to anyone's library."
— *Doody's Health Science Book Reviews, Jan '98*

". . . provide[s] introductory information from the best authorities around. Since this volume covers topics that potentially affect everyone, it will surely be one of the most frequently consulted volumes in the *Health Reference Series*."   — *Rettig on Reference, Nov '97*

"Recommended reference source." — *Booklist, Oct '97*

Fitness & Exercise Sourcebook

Basic Information on Fitness and Exercise, Including Fitness Activities for Specific Age Groups, Exercise for People with Specific Medical Conditions, How to Begin a Fitness Program in Running, Walking, Swimming, Cycling, and Other Athletic Activities, and Recent Research in Fitness and Exercise

In Print. Edited by Dan R. Harris. 663 pages. 1996. 0-7808-0186-5. $78.

"A good resource for general readers."
— *Choice, Nov '97*

"The perennial popularity of the topic . . . make this an appealing selection for public libraries."
— *Rettig on Reference, Jun/Jul '97*

Food & Animal Borne Diseases Sourcebook

Basic Information about Diseases That Can Be Spread to Humans through the Ingestion of Contaminated Food or Water or by Contact with Infected Animals and Insects, Such as Botulism, E. Coli, Hepatitis A, Trichinosis, Lyme Disease, and Rabies, Along with Information Regarding Prevention and Treatment Methods, and a Special Section for International Travelers Describing Diseases Such as Cholera, Malaria, Travelers' Diarrhea, and Yellow Fever, and Offering Recommendations for Avoiding Illness

In Print. Edited by Karen Bellenir and Peter D. Dresser. 535 pages. 1995. 0-7808-0033-8. $78.

"Readable and thorough, this valuable resource is highly recommended for all libraries."
— *Academic Library Book Review, Summer '96*

"A comprehensive collection of authoritative information." — *Emergency Medical Services, Oct '95*

Forensic Medicine Sourcebook

Basic Information for the Layperson about Forensic Medicine, Including Crime Scene Investigation, Evidence Collection and Analysis, Expert Testimony, Accident Reconstruction, Autopsies, Ballistics, Craniofacial Identification, Fingerprinting, DNA Profiling, Handwriting Analysis, and Establishing Paternity, Along with Statistical Data, a Glossary, and Listings of Sources for Further Help and Information

Ready February '99. Edited by Annemarie Muth. Approx. 600 pages. 0-7808-0230-6. $78.

Gastrointestinal Diseases & Disorders Sourcebook

Basic Information about Gastroesophageal Reflux Disease (Heartburn), Ulcers, Diverticulosis, Irritable Bowel Syndrome, Crohn's Disease, Ulcerative Colitis, Diarrhea, Constipation, Lactose Intolerance, Hemorrhoids, Hepatitis, Cirrhosis, and Other Digestive Problems, Featuring Statistics, Descriptions of Symptoms, and Current Treatment Methods of Interest for Persons Living with Upper and Lower Gastrointestinal Maladies

In Print. Edited by Linda M. Ross. 413 pages. 1996. 0-7808-0078-8. $78.

". . . very readable form. The successful editorial work that brought this material together into a useful and understandable reference makes accessible to all readers information that can help them more effectively understand and obtain help for digestive tract problems."   — *Choice, Feb '97*

Genetic Disorders Sourcebook

Basic Information about Heritable Diseases and Disorders Such as Down Syndrome, PKU, Hemophilia, Von Willebrand Disease, Gaucher Disease, Tay-Sachs Disease, and Sickle-Cell Disease, Along with Information about Genetic Screening, Gene Therapy, Home Care, and Including Source Listings for Further Help and Information on More Than 300 Disorders

In Print. Edited by Karen Bellenir. 642 pages. 1996. 0-7808-0034-6. $78.

"Provides essential medical information to both the general public and those diagnosed with a serious or fatal genetic disease or disorder." — *Choice, Jan '97*

". . . geared toward the lay public. It would be well placed in all public libraries and in those hospital and medical libraries in which access to genetic references is limited."
— *Doody's Health Sciences Book Review, Oct '96*

Head Trauma Sourcebook

Basic Information for the Layperson about Open-Head and Closed-Head Injuries, Treatment Advances, Recovery, and Rehabilitation, Along with Reports on Current Research Initiatives

In Print. Edited by Karen Bellenir. 414 pages. 1997. 0-7808-0208-X. $78.

Health Insurance Sourcebook

Basic Information about Managed Care Organizations, Traditional Fee-for-Service Insurance, Insurance Portability and Pre-Existing Conditions Clauses, Medicare, Medicaid, Social Security, and Military Health Care, Along with Information about Insurance Fraud

In Print. Edited by Wendy Wilcox. 530 pages. 1997. 0-7808-0222-5. $78.

"The layout of the book is particularly helpful as it provides easy access to reference material. A most useful addition to the vast amount of information about health insurance. The use of data from U.S. government agencies is most commendable. Useful in a library or learning center for healthcare professional students."
— *Doody's Health Sciences Book Reviews, Nov '97*

Immune System Disorders Sourcebook

Basic Information about Lupus, Multiple Sclerosis, Guillain-Barré Syndrome, Chronic Granulomatous Disease, and More, Along with Statistical and Demographic Data and Reports on Current Research Initiatives

In Print. Edited by Allan R. Cook. 608 pages. 1997. 0-7808-0209-8. $78.

Kidney & Urinary Tract Diseases & Disorders Sourcebook

Basic Information about Kidney Stones, Urinary Incontinence, Bladder Disease, End Stage Renal Disease, Dialysis, and More, Along with Statistical and Demographic Data and Reports on Current Research Initiatives

In Print. Edited by Linda M. Ross. 602 pages. 1997. 0-7808-0079-6. $78.

10% Discount on Health Reference Series Standing Orders — $70.20 per volume.

Fax Orders: 800-875-1340 24 Hours a Day, 7 Days a Week

Learning Disabilities Sourcebook

Basic Information about Disorders Such as Dyslexia, Visual and Auditory Processing Deficits, Attention Deficit/Hyperactivity Disorder, and Autism, Along with Statistical and Demographic Data, Reports on Current Research Initiatives, an Explanation of the Assessment Process, and a Special Section for Adults with Learning Disabilities

In Print. Edited by Linda M. Shin. 579 pages. 1998. 0-7808-0210-1. $78.

Medical Ethics Sourcebook

Basic Information about Controversial Treatment Issues, Genetic Research, Reproductive Technologies, and End-of-Life Decisions, Including Topics Such as Cloning, Abortion, Fertility Management, Organ Transplantation, Health Care Rationing, Advance Directives, Living Wills, Physician-Assisted Suicide, Euthanasia, and More; Along with a Glossary and Resources for Additional Information

Ready December '99. Edited by Helene Henderson. Approx. 600 pages. 0-7808-0237-3. $78.

Men's Health Concerns Sourcebook

Basic Information about Health Issues That Affect Men, Featuring Facts about the Top Causes of Death in Men, Including Heart Disease, Stroke, Cancers, Prostate Disorders, Chronic Obstructive Pulmonary Disease, Pneumonia and Influenza, Human Immunodeficiency Virus and Acquired Immune Deficiency Syndrome, Diabetes Mellitus, Stress, Suicide, Accidents and Homicides; and Facts about Common Concerns for Men, Including Impotence, Contraception, Circumcision, Sleep Disorders, Snoring, Hair Loss, Diet, Nutrition, Exercise, Kidney and Urological Disorders, and Backaches

In Print. Edited by Allan R. Cook. 760 pages. 1998. 0-7808-0212-8. $78.

Mental Health Disorders Sourcebook

Basic Information about Schizophrenia, Depression, Bipolar Disorder, Panic Disorder, Obsessive-Compulsive Disorder, Phobias and Other Anxiety Disorders, Paranoia and Other Personality Disorders, Eating Disorders, and Sleep Disorders, Along with Information about Treatment and Therapies

In Print. Edited by Karen Bellenir. 548 pages. 1995. 0-7808-0040-0. $78.

"This is an excellent new book . . . written in easy-to-understand language."
— Booklist Health Science Supplement, Oct '97

". . . useful for public and academic libraries and consumer health collections."
— Medical Reference Services Quarterly, Spring '97

"The great strengths of the book are its readability and its inclusion of places to find more information. Especially recommended."
— RQ, Winter '96

". . . a good resource for a consumer health library."
— Bulletin of the MLA, Oct '96

"The text is well organized and adequately written for its target audience."
— Choice, Jun '96

"Recommended for public and academic libraries."
— Reference Book Review, '96

Neurological Disorders Sourcebook

Basic Information about Non-Dementing Neurological Disorders, Including Stroke and Post-Stroke Rehabilitation, Epilepsy and Other Seizure-Inducing Disorders, Multiple Sclerosis, Cerebral Palsy, Tourette Syndrome, Brain Injuries and Tumors, Amyotrophic Lateral Sclerosis (ALS), and More; Along with Statistical and Demographic Data, Treatment Options, Coping Strategies, Reports on Current Research Initiatives, a Glossary, and Resource Listings for Additional Help and Information

Ready March '99. Edited by Karen Bellenir. Approx. 600 pages. 0-7808-0229-2. $78.

Ophthalmic Disorders Sourcebook

Basic Information about Glaucoma, Cataracts, Macular Degeneration, Strabismus, Refractive Disorders, and More, Along with Statistical and Demographic Data and Reports on Current Research Initiatives

In Print. Edited by Linda M. Ross. 631 pages. 1996. 0-7808-0081-8. $78.

Oral Health Sourcebook

Basic Information about Diseases and Conditions Affecting Oral Health, Including Cavities, Gum Disease, Dry Mouth, Oral Cancers, Fever Blisters, Canker Sores, Oral Thrush, Bad Breath, Temporomandibular Disorders, and other Craniofacial Syndromes, Along with Statistical Data on the Oral Health of Americans, Oral Hygiene, Emergency First Aid, Information on Treatment Procedures and Methods of Replacing Lost Teeth

In Print. Edited by Allan R. Cook. 558 pages. 1997. 0-7808-0082-6. $78.

"Recommended reference source." — Booklist, Dec '97

Pain Sourcebook

Basic Information about Specific Forms of Acute and Chronic Pain, Including Headaches, Back Pain, Muscular Pain, Neuralgia, Surgical Pain, and Cancer Pain, Along with Pain Relief Options Such as Analgesics, Narcotics, Nerve Blocks, Transcutaneous Nerve Stimulation, and Alternative Forms of Pain Control, Including Biofeedback, Imaging, Behavior Modification, and Relaxation Techniques

In Print. Edited by Allan R. Cook. 667 pages. 1997. 0-7808-0213-6. $78.

"The information is basic in terms of scholarship and is appropriate for general readers. Written in journalistic style . . . intended for non-professionals. Quite thorough in its coverage of different pain conditions and summarizes the latest clinical information regarding pain treatment."
— Choice, Jun '98

"Recommended reference source."
— Booklist, Mar '98

Pregnancy & Birth Sourcebook

Basic Information about Planning for Pregnancy, Maternal Health, Fetal Growth and Development, Labor and Delivery, Postpartum and Perinatal Care, Pregnancy in Mothers with Special Concerns, and Disorders of Pregnancy, Including Genetic Counseling, Nutrition and Exercise, Obstetrical Tests, Pregnancy Discomfort, Multiple Births, Cesarean Sections, Medical Testing of Newborns, Breastfeeding, Gestational Diabetes, and Ectopic Pregnancy

In Print. Edited by Heather E. Aldred. 737 pages. 1997. 0-7808-0216-0. $78.

". . . for the layperson. A well-organized handbook. Recommended for college libraries . . . general readers."
— Choice, Apr '98

"Recommended reference source."
— Booklist, Mar '98

"This resource is recommended for public libraries to have on hand."
— American Reference Books Annual, '98

Public Health Sourcebook

Basic Information about Government Health Agencies, Including National Health Statistics and Trends, Healthy People 2000 Program Goals and Objectives, the Centers for Disease Control and Prevention, the Food and Drug Administration, and the National Institutes of Health, Along with Full Contact Information for Each Agency

In Print. Edited by Wendy Wilcox. 698 pages. 1998. 0-7808-0220-9. $78.

RehabilitationSourcebook

Basic Information for the Layperson about Physical Medicine (Physiatry) and Rehabilitative Therapies, Including Physical, Occupational, Recreational, Speech, and Vocational Therapy; Along with Descriptions of Devices and Equipment Such as Orthotics, Gait Aids, Prostheses, and Adaptive Systems Used during Rehabilitation and for Activities of Daily Living, and Featuring a Glossary and Source Listings for Further Help and Information

Ready March '99. Edited by Theresa K. Murray. Approx. 600 pages. 0-7808-0236-5. $78.

Respiratory Diseases & Disorders Sourcebook

Basic Information about Respiratory Diseases and Disorders, Including Asthma, Cystic Fibrosis, Pneumonia, the Common Cold, Influenza, and Others, Featuring Facts about the Respiratory System, Statistical and Demographic Data, Treatments, Self-Help Management Suggestions, and Current Research Initiatives

In Print. Edited by Allan R. Cook and Peter D. Dresser. 771 pages. 1995. 0-7808-0037-0. $78.

"Designed for the layperson and for patients and their families coping with respiratory illness. . . . an extensive array of information on diagnosis, treatment, management, and prevention of respiratory illnesses for the general reader." — *Choice, Jun '96*

"A highly recommended text for all collections. It is a comforting reminder of the power of knowledge that good books carry between their covers." — *Academic Library Book Review, Spring '96*

"This sourcebook offers a comprehensive collection of authoritative information presented in a nontechnical, humanitarian style for patients, families, and caregivers." — *Association of Operating Room Nurses, Sept/Oct '95*

Fax Orders: 800-875-1340
24 Hours a Day 7 Days a Week

Sexually Transmitted Diseases Sourcebook

Basic Information about Herpes, Chlamydia, Gonorrhea, Hepatitis, Nongonoccocal Urethritis, Pelvic Inflammatory Disease, Syphilis, AIDS, and More, Along with Current Data on Treatments and Preventions

In Print. Edited by Linda M. Ross. 550 pages. 1997. 0-7808-0217-9. $78.

Skin Disorders Sourcebook

Basic Information about Common Skin and Scalp Conditions Caused by Aging, Allergies, Immune Reactions, Sun Exposure, Infectious Organisms, Parasites, Cosmetics, and Skin Traumas, Including Abrasions, Cuts, and Pressure Sores, Along with Information on Prevention and Treatment

In Print. Edited by Allan R. Cook. 647 pages. 1997. 0-7808-0080-X. $78.

". . . comprehensive easily read reference book." — *Doody's Health Sciences Book Reviews, Oct '97*

Sleep Disorders Sourcebook

Basic Consumer Health Information about Sleep and Its Disorders, Including Insomnia, Sleepwalking, Sleep Apnea, Restless Leg Syndrome, and Narcolepsy; Along with Data about Shiftwork and Its Effects, Information on the Societal Costs of Sleep Deprivation, Descriptions of Treatment Options, a Glossary of Terms, and Resource Listings for Additional Help

In Print. Edited by Jenifer Swanson. 475 pages. 1998. 0-7808-0234-9. $78.

Sports Injuries Sourcebook

Basic Information about Common Sports Injuries, Prevention of Injury in Specific Sports, Tips for Training, and Rehabilitation from Injury; Along with Special Sections on Concerns for Young Girls in Athletic Training Programs, Senior Athletes, and Women Athletes, a Glossary, and Source Listings for Further Help and Information

Ready January '99. Edited by Heather Aldred. Approx. 600 pages. 0-7808-0218-7. $78.

10% Discount on Health Reference Series Standing Orders — $70.20 per volume.

Fax Orders: 800-875-1340 24 Hours a Day, 7 Days a Week Phone Orders: 800-234-1340

Substance Abuse Sourcebook

Basic Health-Related Information about the Abuse of Legal and Illegal Substances Such as Alcohol, Tobacco, Prescription Drugs, Marijuana, Cocaine, and Heroin; and Including Facts about Substance Abuse Prevention Strategies, Intervention Methods, Treatment and Recovery Programs, and a Section Addressing the Special Problems Related to Substance Abuse during Pregnancy

In Print. Edited by Karen Bellenir. 573 pages. 1996. 0-7808-0038-9. $78.

"A valuable addition to any health reference section. Highly recommended."

— *The Book Report, Mar/Apr '97*

". . . a comprehensive collection of substance abuse information that's both highly readable and compact. Families and caregivers of substance abusers will find the information enlightening and helpful, while teachers, social workers and journalists should benefit from the concise format. Recommended."

— *Drug Abuse Update, Winter '96-'97*

Women's Health Concerns Sourcebook

Basic Information about Health Issues That Affect Women, Featuring Facts about Menstruation and Other Gynecological Concerns, Including Endometriosis, Fibroids, Menopause, and Vaginitis; Reproductive Concerns, Including Birth Control, Infertility, and Abortion; and Facts about Additional Physical, Emotional, and Mental Health Concerns Prevalent among Women Such as Osteoporosis, Urinary Tract Disorders, Eating Disorders, and Depression, Along with Tips for Maintaining a Healthy Lifestyle

In Print. Edited by Heather Aldred. 567 pages. 1997. ISBN 0-7808-0219-5. $78.

"Handy compilation. There is an impressive range of diseases, devices, disorders, procedures, and other physical and emotional issues covered . . . well organized, illustrated, and indexed."

— *Choice, Jan '98*

Workplace Health & Safety Sourcebook

Basic Information about Musculoskeletal Injuries, Cumulative Trauma Disorders, Occupational Carcinogens and Other Toxic Materials, Child Labor, Workplace Violence, Histoplasmosis, Transmission of HIV and Hepatitis-B Viruses, and Occupational Hazards Associated with Various Industries, Including Mining, Confined Spaces, Agriculture, Construction, Electrical Work, and the Medical Professions, with Information on Mortality and Other Statistical Data, Preventative Measures, Reproductive Risks, Reducing Stress for Shiftworkers, Noise Hazards, Industrial Back Belts, Reducing Contamination at Home, Preventing Allergic Reactions to Rubber Latex, and More; Along with Public and Private Programs and Initiatives, a Glossary, and Sources for Additional Help and Information

Ready July '99. Edited by Helene Henderson. Approx. 600 pages. 0-7808-0231-4. $78.

Announcing the Expanded
Health Reference Series . . .

"Taken as a whole, this series provides a condensed, centralized source of information unmatched in scope and usefulness for the general reading audience."

— *Academic Library Book Review,*
Summer '96

Call 800-234-1340
to request a free copy of the new 1999 catalog for the *Health Reference Series*

This 32-page catalog provides full listings with descriptions of all 58 volumes. Sample pages — charts, tables, illustrations, indexes, and general layout and format — illustrate at a glance, the kind of quality you can expect to see in each individual volume. The *Health Reference Series* is a first-stop medical library for the general reader.

Featuring:

9 All-New Subject Volumes

Aging Body Sourcebook
Death & Dying Sourcebook
Domestic Violence Sourcebook
Forensic Medicine Sourcebook
Medical Ethics Sourcebook
Neurological Disorders Sourcebook
Rehabilitation Sourcebook
Sleep Disorders Sourcebook
Workplace Health & Safety Sourcebook

6 New Editions

AIDS Sourcebook, 2nd Edition
Alzheimer's Disease Sourcebook,
    2nd Edition
Cancer Sourcebook, 3rd Edition
Cancer Sourcebook for Women, 2nd Edition
Diabetes Sourcebook, 2nd Edition
Diet & Nutrition Sourcebook, 2nd Edition

3 Forthcoming Titles

Alternative Medicine Sourcebook
Burns Sourcebook
Sports Injuries Sourcebook

8 Titles Just Published

Arthritis Sourcebook
Blood & Circulatory Disorders Sourcebook
Consumer Issues in Health Care
Ear, Nose & Throat Disorders Sourcebook
Endocrine & Metabolic Disorders
    Sourcebook
Learning Disabilities Sourcebook
Men's Health Concerns Sourcebook
Public Health Sourcebook

Health Reference Series 60-Day On-Approval Order Form

Enter our order for the following volumes:

Forthcoming Titles

Recently Published Titles

Now In Print Titles

SERIES STANDING ORDER — 10% DISCOUNT

___ Enter a Standing Order for the *Health Reference Series* .... $70.20 per volume

A Standing Order is an automatic renewal. Enter a Standing Order to receive each new edition upon publication, less a 10% discount.

❑ Payment enclosed,
  ship postpaid

❑ Bill us, plus shipping (libraries, schools,
  and government agencies only)

Omnigraphics, Inc.

Penobscot Building
Detroit, MI 48226

Fax Orders: 800-875-1340
24 Hours a Day, 7 Days a Week
Phone Orders: 800-234-1340

Organization _____

Name_____

Title_____

Address _____

City_____

State_____ Zip_____

Phone (_____)_____